Great Grandma Dot

Written by
Laura Appleton-Smith

Illustrated by
Keinyo White

Laura Appleton-Smith holds a degree in English from Middlebury College.
Laura is a primary school teacher who has combined her talents in creative writing with
her experience in early childhood education to create *Books to Remember*.
She lives in New Hampshire with her husband, Terry.

Keinyo White is a graduate of the Rhode Island School of Design with a B.F.A. in illustration.
He currently produces children's books and freelance illustrations
from his studio in Los Angeles.

A Book to Remember™
Published by Flyleaf Publishing

For orders or information, contact us at **(800) 449-7006**.
Please visit our website at **www.flyleafpublishing.com**

Eighth Edition 2/20
Library of Congress Catalog Card Number: 2009937032
ISBN-13: 978-1-60541-018-0
Printed and bound in the USA at Worzalla Publishing, Stevens Point, WI

In memory of my Grandma Tosh, Grandma Phil, and my Mommy Jan.

LAS

For Scarlett and Ajani.

KW

I am 7. My Great Grandma Dot is 87.
Grandma Dot is my mom's mom's mom.

Grandma Dot is different and fun.
She loves dresses with vivid patterns.
And she loves her hot-pink slippers.

4

Grandma Dot has lots of love.

When I visit her I run up her steps to get a big hug.

Grandma Dot's soft skin smells of talc and lavender.

Grandma Dot loves red lipstick,
and she loves to plant kisses.
"I just love you to bits," she tells me
as she dots me with red lipstick spots.

Muffins crisp in Grandma Dot's oven
and grits simmer in her pan.
Grandma Dot tends to a skillet
filled with sizzling drumsticks.

Grandma Dot loves to fill me up.
Supper is a big drumstick and lots of yummy food.

After supper, I love to help Grandma Dot.
We fill the sink with suds and scrub her pots and pans.
Bubbles drift and pop in the kitchen.

"If you have to scrub," she tells me,
"it is just as well to have a bit of fun!"

14

After scrubbing the dishes, Grandma Dot sits and quilts scraps of fabric into blankets.

"This denim fabric is a bit of Great Grandpop's jacket," she tells me. "Quilts are scraps of the past put into blankets that are vivid and new."

16

I tuck in next to Grandma Dot.

She hums soft songs as she rocks the rocker.

I drift off as if I am a bubble from
the suds in Grandma Dot's sink.

I understand that I am loved,
and I understand that Great Grandma Dot is great.

Prerequisite Skills

Single consonants and short vowels
Final double consonants **ff**, **gg**, **ll**, **nn**, **ss**, **tt**, **zz**
Consonant /k/ **ck**
/ng/ **n[k]**
Consonant digraphs /ng/ **ng**, /th/ **th**, /hw/ **wh**
Schwa /ə/ **a**, **e**, **i**, **o**, **u**
Long /ē/ **ee**, **y**
r-Controlled /ûr/ **er**
/ô/ **al**, **all**
/ul/ **le**
/d/ or /t/ **–ed**

Target Letter-Sound Correspondence

Foundational Skills
Consolidation

Story Puzzle Words

Grandma	loved
kitchen	loves
love	oven

High-Frequency Puzzle Words

are	new
food	of
from	put
great	she
have	to
into	we
me	you
my	

Decodable Words

7	Dot	hot	next	scrubbing	tends
87	Dot's	hug	off	simmer	that
a	dots	hums	pan	sink	the
after	dresses	I	pans	sits	this
am	drift	if	past	sizzling	tuck
and	drumstick	in	patterns	skillet	understand
as	drumsticks	is	pink	skin	up
big	fabric	it	plant	slippers	visit
bit	fill	jacket	pop	smells	vivid
bits	filled	just	pots	soft	well
blankets	fun	kisses	quilts	songs	when
bubble	get	lavender	red	spots	with
bubbles	Grandpop's	lipstick	rocker	steps	yummy
crisp	grits	lots	rocks	suds	
denim	has	mom	run	supper	
different	help	mom's	scraps	talc	
dishes	her	muffins	scrub	tells	